This Walker book belongs to:

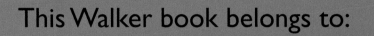

....

....

For Terry and Ana
NS

For Daisy and Harry
SS

First published 2010 by Walker Books Ltd
87 Vauxhall Walk, London SE11 5HJ

This edition published 2011 for Bookstart

2 4 6 8 10 9 7 5 3 1

Text © 2010 Sally Symes and Nick Sharratt
Illustrations © 2010 Nick Sharratt

This book has been typeset in Gill Sans

Printed in China

British Library Cataloguing in Publication Data:
a catalogue record for this book is available from the British Library

ISBN 978-1-4063-3100-4

www.walker.co.uk

Something Beginning with
BLUE

Nick
Sharratt

Sally
Symes

WALKER BOOKS
AND SUBSIDIARIES

LONDON · BOSTON · SYDNEY · AUCKLAND

I spy with my little eye,
something beginning with ...
blue.

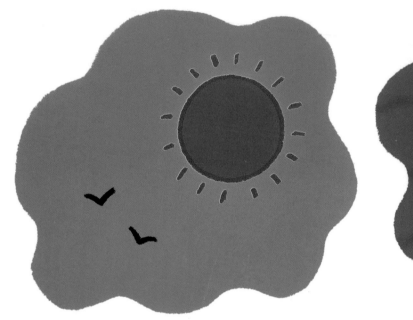

It isn't blue sky and it isn't blue sea.

It's five hundred and fifty times
bigger than me...

A blue
whale!

I spy with my little eye,

something beginning with ...

green.

It's not one of these

and it's not one of those.

It's got tough, scaly skin and blows
smoke through its nose...

A green
dragon!

I spy with my little eye,

something beginning with ...

grey.

It doesn't eat cheese.

It might like some hay.

If it started to **charge**

I'd get out of the way (fast!)...

A grey rhinoceros!

I spy with my little eye,
something beginning with ...
brown.

It's not chocolate buttons.

It's not a brown owl.

It's got lovely soft fur,
but a really **fierce** growl...

A brown bear!

I spy with my little eye,
something beginning with ...
black.

It's not a black bird.

It's not a black cat.

It has eight wriggling legs
and is hairy and fat...

A black spider!

We spy with our little eyes,

something beginning with …

yummy!

It's

bursting with all of

the **colours** you see…

Can you guess
what it is?

It's our
fancy
dress tea!

Also by **Nick Sharratt** and **Sally Symes**

978-1-4063-3082-3

Other books by **Nick Sharratt**

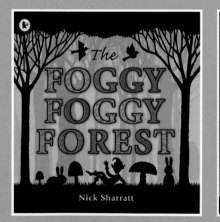

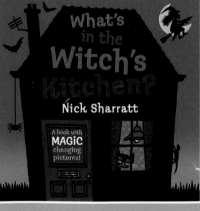

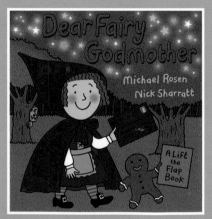

978-1-4063-2784-7   978-1-4063-2227-9   978-1-4063-2557-7   978-1-4063-1832-6

Available from all good bookstores

www.walker.co.uk